SUMMER

LANDMARK EDITIONS, INC.

P.O. Box 270169 • 1402 Kansas Avenue • Kansas City, Missouri 64127

(816)241-4919

DISCOVERY

WRITTEN AND ILLUSTRATED BY
DREW CARSON

Dedicated to
my mom and dad
who love and encourage me;

to my buddy, Carl;

and to Levi because
he will always be my friend
and because he taught me
how to build forts.

With a special thank you to
Isaac Barner, Archaeologist,
Roseburg District
Bureau of Land Management.

COPYRIGHT © 1998 BY DREW CARSON

International Standard Book Number: 0-933849-68-0 (LIB.BDG.)

Library of Congress Cataloging-in-Publication Data
Carson, Drew, 1988-
    Summer discovery / written and illustrated by Drew Carson.
    p. cm.
    Summary: While building a fort near their homes by Oregon's
Umpqua River, two nine-year-olds make a discovery that involves their
neighbors in trying to stop a bridge from being built on an important
archaeological site.
  ISBN 0-933849-68-0 (lib.bdg. : alk. paper)
  1. Children's writings, American.
  [1. Paleontology—Fiction.   2. Fossils—Fiction.
  3. Neighbors—Fiction.   4. Children's writings.]
  I. Title.
  PZ7.C2385Su   1998
  [Fic]--dc21   98-13429
                                  CIP
                                  AC

Creative Coordinator: David Melton
Editorial Coordinator: Nancy R. Thatch
Production Assistant: Brian Hubbard

Printed in the United States of America

Landmark Editions, Inc.
P.O. Box 270169
1402 Kansas Avenue
Kansas City, Missouri 64127
(816) 241-4919

Visit our Website — www.LandmarkEditions.com

SUMMER DISCOVERY

Readers of all ages should be able to identify with the problems of the two central characters in this book. Two nine-year-old boys, Drew and Carl, have made a "super plan" for the summer, but bad weather and a series of incidents force them to change those plans. Because of the changes, the boys make some unusual discoveries, and new and even more exciting adventures begin to unfold for them.

SUMMER DISCOVERY is a very interesting story, told in a very interesting way. Drew thoroughly understands his central characters, who are named Drew and Carl after the young author and his real-life friend, Carl. The boys live in the same neighborhood by the banks of the South Umpqua River in Roseburg, Oregon. And they have spent a number of summers together, playing and exploring, and building makeshift forts from sticks and debris that have washed ashore.

SUMMER DISCOVERY is a wonderful example for children to see and read because it demonstrates how writers can take real-life experiences, add fictional events, and turn them into exciting stories.

Drew's illustrations are truly outstanding, especially for a nine-year-old. They are greatly improved from the ones he painted for his original book. While Drew was preparing his final illustrations for publication, I was delighted to see his drawing and painting skills improve by more than four grade levels. The growth he made as an artist was exciting for him to see, too, which is the way it should be when people learn new things.

I loved working with Drew and discussing his illustrations with him and his parents. Like most of the parents of our authors and illustrators, both his mother and father were very helpful in scheduling Drew's time and encouraging him during his extraordinary creative experience.

The result of Drew's imagination and skills as a writer and an artist is a thoughtfully plotted, exciting story, with wonderfully constructed and beautifully painted illustrations.

Now you are invited to join Drew and Carl. It's their last day of school, and summer vacation is about to begin...

— David Melton
Creative Coordinator
Landmark Editions, Inc.

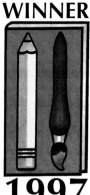

WINNER

1997
WRITTEN &
ILLUSTRATED
BY... AWARD

It was the last day of school. *Hooray!*

My best friend, Carl, and I were really excited. As soon as the bell rang, we grabbed our backpacks. Then we called good-bye to our third-grade teacher and hurried out the door.

We were the first ones to climb aboard the school bus. We sat down quickly. As Carl cleaned his glasses, we began talking.

We certainly had plenty to talk about. Carl and I had a SUPER PLAN for the summer. We could hardly wait to get home and get started.

When we got off the bus, Carl said, "I'll race you to your house!"

"You're on!" I laughed. "Let's go!"

It was a close race, and both of us yelled, "I won!" But that didn't matter. We had more important things to do.

"I'm home," I called to my mom. Then Carl and I dropped our backpacks on the porch and hurried to the garage. We soon found a couple of shovels, a saw, a hammer, and a big box of nails. We loaded them into an old, rusty wheelbarrow that creaked loudly as we pushed it out of the garage. We had everything we needed to put our SUPER PLAN into action.

"See you first thing in the morning," Carl said.

"I'll be ready," I told him.

The big day Carl and I had been waiting for all year finally arrived. I woke up early, got dressed, and rushed outside.

Carl was already there, waiting for me.

"Good morning," he said cheerfully.

"It's more than just a *good* morning. It's a *great* morning!" I exclaimed. "Let's get started!"

Together, we pushed the creaking wheelbarrow down the slope that led to the bank of the Umpqua River.

Our SUPER PLAN was to build a fort on this slope that overlooked

the river. It was a perfect place for a fort, but it wouldn't be perfect for long. In August the city planned to build a bridge from our bank to the other side of the river.

None of our neighbors liked the idea of the bridge being built so close to their houses. Carl and I didn't like it either, because it would destroy the fort we planned to build.

But bridge or no bridge, Carl and I were determined to build our fort on the spot we had chosen. And we were going to enjoy it for as long as we could.

What a grand fort it was going to be!

With our shovels, we marked off the square area on the ground where our fort would stand. Then we started clearing away the grass that grew inside the space. By noon we had finished. After lunch we began digging the holes for the four corner posts.

But in late afternoon, dark clouds gathered, and the rain *really* poured! We threw our tools into the wheelbarrow and pushed it up the hill. By the time we reached my garage, we were soaking wet!

"See you tomorrow," we said as we ran toward our houses.

The next morning when I awoke, I could still hear rain pounding on the roof. I put on a raincoat and my boots, then ran next door to Carl's house. He was glad to see me.

We decided to make a fort in his basement. We draped blankets over a table and some chairs. It was fun. But our inside fort wasn't nearly as good as the one we were going to build outside.

In the afternoon we watched cartoons and listened to it rain. It was like being trapped inside of a house that was under a waterfall.

Guess what? It rained the next day, too.

On the fourth morning, there wasn't a cloud in sight. The sun shone brightly. The sky was dry, but the ground was wet and very muddy. Carl and I had to wear our boots. We sloshed and slid as we pushed the wheelbarrow down to the site for our fort.

"Look," Carl said, "our fort is a swimming pool!"

He was right. The rain had washed away a lot of dirt from the square area where we had removed the grass. Now there was a hole that was at least a foot deep. And it was filled with water!

We took our shovels and dug a trench so the water would drain out. We cheered as we watched the water flow down the bank.

The water had left a thick layer of mud in the bottom of the hole. Shoveling out that heavy mud was really hard work!

As we shoveled we noticed something was sparkling in the mud. It looked like tiny pieces of shiny rock. We wiped some of them off and put them in our pockets.

That evening we showed them to my dad.

"They're flakes of obsidian rock," he said. "Indians used to make arrowheads out of it. These are flakes they chipped off."

"Maybe we'll find some of those arrowheads," I said.

"That would really be cool," agreed Carl.

The next morning we hurried to the site. Although we dug for a long time, we didn't find any arrowheads. Then my shovel scraped against something hard. I pushed the blade of the shovel under the object and pried it out.

How disappointing! It was only an oval-shaped rock. But it looked different from other rocks. I decided to save it, so I tossed it into the wheelbarrow.

I dug some more. After awhile my shovel struck something else. I kept shoveling until I had uncovered a large stone. I tried to pull it out of the mud. I couldn't.

"Hey, Carl," I called, "Come here and help me lift this thing."

Carl came over, and we pulled and pulled. Suddenly the heavy

stone slipped out of the mud, and Carl and I fell backwards.

It was really a strange looking stone. It was flat on one side and there was a smooth, hollowed-out area on the other.

"It looks like the inside of a bowl," Carl said.

We loaded our strange stone into the wheelbarrow next to the oval rock. Then we pushed it up the hill.

"Dad," I called, "Come and see what we found."

My dad hurried outside. He inspected the oval rock. And then he rubbed his hands over the bowl-shaped surface of the large stone.

"These are quite unusual," he said. "Where did you find them?"

"Where we were digging," I answered.

"I think we should show them to an archaeologist," Dad said.

Several days later my dad took us to see an archaeologist who lived in our area. Professor Lee's office was very interesting. Books and maps, and even some bones were on his desk.

The professor was a very friendly man. He carefully examined the stone and the rock. Then he peered at us over his glasses.

"The large stone is a mortar," he said. "The oval rock is a pestle."

"What are they used for?" I asked.

"For grinding," he replied. "The Indians used to place nuts and dried berries in the hollowed-out area of the mortar. Then they would use the pestle to grind them up."

"We found these, too," I said as I placed some of the flakes of obsidian in his hand.

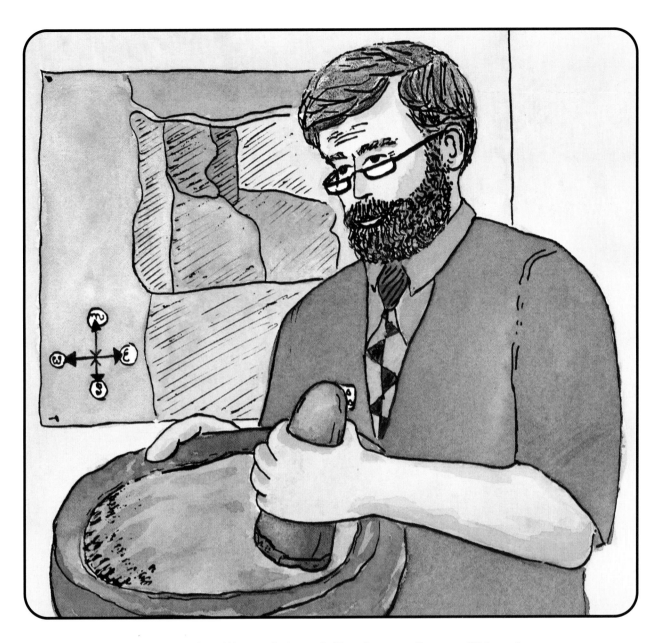

"Very interesting!" exclaimed Professor Lee. "You boys may have found an old campsite, used by Indians when they were on their way to hunt. Or you may have dug into the remains of an Umpqua Indian village. If it's a village, the two of you have made an important archaeological discovery."

Carl and I smiled proudly.

"I would like to send one of my assistants to look at the site," said Professor Lee.

"You had better do it quickly," my dad told him. "In August the city plans to start building a bridge across that area."

"If it becomes an important archaeological site," Professor Lee replied, "no one will build a bridge there."

Professor Lee's assistant arrived at my house early the next day. Her name was Maggie. Carl and I led her to our digging site. We couldn't help but feel a little important.

As Maggie examined the area, Carl and I just stood back and watched. When she started digging, we saw she was very careful. We noticed that she was using a smaller shovel than we had.

The ground had dried out a lot by now, so Maggie could sift the dirt, too. She would drop a shovelful into a wooden box that had a screen on the bottom. When she shook the box back and forth, only the dirt would sift through the screen.

"This is the way we find arrowheads and other small objects," Maggie explained.

"Say, would you boys like to help me sift?" she asked.

"We sure would!" we replied eagerly.

We felt like real archaeologists as we shook the box and watched the dirt sift through. At first we didn't find anything except pebbles. Then we found some arrowheads — three of them! We were thrilled! We stored them in a small, clear plastic bag.

That afternoon our neighbor, Jack, came down to see what was going on. Jack was a nice man and a good friend. When Carl and I told him what we were doing, he offered to help us dig.

"Great!" said Carl. "We need lots of help. We must find something important here so the city won't build that bridge."

Jack rolled up his sleeves, picked up a shovel, and started digging.

Jack told other neighbors about our archaeological site. So every day many of them, including our parents, came to help.

One day Professor Lee stopped by to see what progress we had made. He looked at the few arrowheads we had found.

"This may only be a campsite," he said. "So don't get your hopes up too high. A simple campsite is not enough to stop the bridge from being built."

Even so, none of us wanted to give up. All day long for the next two months, we dug and we sifted. Before we went home each evening, we had to spread a heavy tarp over the excavated area in case it might rain.

On the first day of August, Professor Lee came back to the site and talked to us. He told us we had done a wonderful job. He said he had never had better workers. Then he turned to Carl and me.

"I'm sorry, boys," he said, shaking his head sadly, "but you have not found enough artifacts to prove that this was an Indian village. I believe this was only a campsite."

Carl and I hung our heads in disappointment. All of us had done so much work and found just a little campsite! Everyone else was disappointed, too.

After the others had gone home, Carl and I helped Maggie spread the tarp over the site.

Later that day bulldozers rumbled onto the slope. They stopped and sat there like monsters, ready to chew up the earth.

But before the drivers could start working, the weather changed. Dark clouds rolled across the sky and gusts of wind blew. Lightning flashed and thunder roared. And then it started to rain, not just a little rain, but a real downpour!

"Well," said Carl, "at least the rain stopped the bulldozers."

"Not for long," I said. "They're still up there, ready to attack."

The storm lasted all night long. Carl and I didn't know it then, but that storm would change our lives.

When Carl and I got to the site the next morning, we found that

the wind had blown away the tarp. The pouring rain had caused a giant mud slide to plunge all the way down to the river.

Then we noticed something that looked very strange. There were a lot of large gray things lying in the mud.

"What are those?" I asked.

"They look like bones," Carl replied.

"That's what they are!" I exclaimed. "They *are* bones!"

We ran back to my house and phoned Professor Lee.

"Hello, Professor," I said excitedly. "I think you should come over here right away. Carl and I just found some things you have to see. And they are big. How big? REALLY BIG!"

As we waited the bulldozers started to rumble. Our neighbors heard the noise and hurried down to the site. In a few minutes, Professor Lee arrived.

When he saw what was in the mud, he gasped in amazement!

"These are the bones of a mammoth!" he exclaimed.

"Are these bones important enough to stop the building of that bridge?" I asked quickly.

"They certainly are!" he replied.

Then we heard the bulldozers roar into high gear.

"Look!" warned Carl. "They're coming down the slope!"

Professor Lee turned and faced the invading machines. The rest of us lined up with him and refused to move out of the way.

We knew we were all that stood between the exposed bones of the mammoth and the approaching bulldozers!

The professor raised his hand. "STOP RIGHT NOW!" he commanded. "You cannot dig here! The bones of a prehistoric animal have just been discovered at this site!"

The bulldozers slowed down, then finally rumbled to a stop.

WE HAD WON!

All of us cheered!

The newspaper headline read —

TWO BOYS FIND MAMMOTH BONES!

Television crews arrived.

"Which one of you found the bones?" a reporter asked.

"We both found them," I replied.

Then Carl and I smiled for the cameras. Pictures of us standing by the bones were printed in magazines and newspapers around the world. We were interviewed on television. Wherever we went people recognized us and asked us for our autographs.

Like it or not, Carl and I were famous. We liked it!

It was our first day back at school. We soon found out that famous or not, we had to do our schoolwork, just like everyone else.

That afternoon we rode the same school bus. We walked to our same houses. And we went down the same slope toward the excavation site. We wanted to see if anything else had been uncovered.

But as we neared the site, something in the distance attracted our attention — something made of logs. We had never seen it before. We wondered what it was.

When we got closer, we could see it was a two-story, wooden building with a lookout tower on top.

"WOW!" exclaimed Carl. "What a neat place!"

"Sure is!" I agreed. "I wonder who it belongs to."

When we got a few feet from it, we found out.
And boy, were we surprised!
The plaque above the door read:

> THIS FORT BELONGS TO CARL AND DREW.
> THANK YOU FOR SAVING OUR NEIGHBORHOOD!
> — YOUR FRIENDS AND NEIGHBORS —

Carl and I finally had our fort on the banks of the Umpqua River. And we played in that fort for many summers.

We often visit the museum where the bones of the mammoth are kept. We will never forget our summer discovery.

"Just think," said Carl, "it all started because we dug a few little holes in the ground."

BOOKS FOR STUDENTS BY STUDENTS!

Left sidebar photos:

Dav Pilkey
age 19

Lauren Peters
age 7

Benjamin Kendall
age 7

Amy Hagstrom
age 9

Michael Cain
age 11

Leslie A. MacKeen
age 9

Shintaro Maeda
age 8

A. Chandrasekhar
age 9

Dennis Vollmer
age 6

Alise Leggat
age 8

by Karen Kerber, age 12
St. Louis, Missouri
ISBN 0-933849-29-X   Full Color

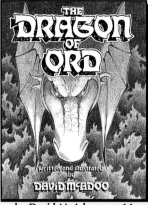

by David McAdoo, age 14
Springfield, Missouri
ISBN 0-933849-23-0   Inside Duotone

by Amy Hagstrom, age 9
Portola, California
ISBN 0-933849-15-X   Full Color

by Isaac Whitlatch, age 1?
Casper, Wyoming
ISBN 0-933849-16-8   Full Color

by Leslie Ann MacKeen, age 9
Winston-Salem, North Carolina
ISBN 0-933849-19-2   Full Color

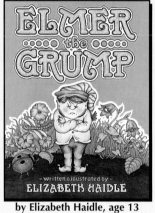

by Elizabeth Haidle, age 13
Beaverton, Oregon
ISBN 0-933849-20-6   Full Color

by Heidi Salter, age 19
Berkeley, California
ISBN 0-933849-21-4   Full Color

by Lauren Peters, age 7
Kansas City, Missouri
ISBN 0-933849-25-7   Full Color

by Aruna Chandrasekhar, age 9
Houston, Texas
ISBN 0-933849-33-8   Full Color

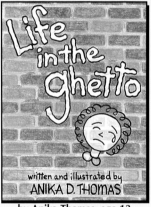

by Anika Thomas, age 13
Pittsburgh, Pennsylvania
ISBN 0-933849-34-6   Inside Two Colors

by Cara Reichel, age 15
Rome, Georgia
ISBN 0-933849-35-4   Inside Two Colors

by Jonathan Kahn, age 9
Richmond Heights, Ohio
ISBN 0-933849-36-2   Full Color

by Benjamin Kendall, age 7
State College, Pennsylvania
ISBN 0-933849-42-7   Full Color

by Steven Shepard, age 13
Great Falls, Virginia
ISBN 0-933849-43-5   Full Color

by Travis Williams, age 16
Sardis, B.C., Canada
ISBN 0-933849-44-3   Inside Two Colors

by Dubravka Kolanović, age
Savannah, Georgia
ISBN 0-933849-45-1   Full Color

THE NATIONAL WRITTEN & ILLUSTRATED BY...AWARD WINNERS

by Dav Pilkey, age 19
Cleveland, Ohio
ISBN 0-933849-22-2   Full Color

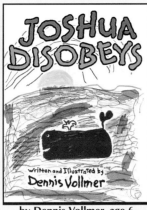
by Dennis Vollmer, age 6
Grove, Oklahoma
ISBN 0-933849-12-5   Full Color

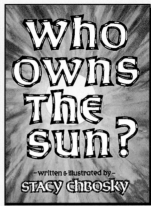
by Lisa Gross, age 12
Santa Fe, New Mexico
ISBN 0-933849-13-3   Full Color

by Stacy Chbosky, age 14
Pittsburgh, Pennsylvania
ISBN 0-933849-14-1   Full Color

by Michael Cain, age 11
Annapolis, Maryland
ISBN 0-933849-26-5   Full Color

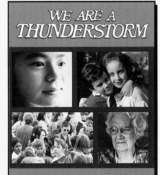
by Amity Gaige, age 16
Reading, Pennsylvania
ISBN 0-933849-27-3   Full Color

by Adam Moore, age 9
Broken Arrow, Oklahoma
ISBN 0-933849-24-9   Inside Duotone

by Michael Aushenker, age 19
Ithaca, New York
ISBN 0-933849-28-1   Full Color

by Jayna Miller, age 19
Zanesville, Ohio
ISBN 0-933849-37-0   Full Color

by Bonnie-Alise Leggat, age 8
Culpepper, Virginia
ISBN 0-933849-39-7   Full Color

by Lisa Kirsten Butenhoff, age 13
Woodbury, Minnesota
ISBN 0-933849-40-0   Full Color

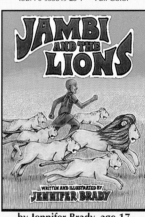
by Jennifer Brady, age 17
Columbia, Missouri
ISBN 0-933849-41-9   Full Color

by Amy Jones, age 17
Shirley, Arkansas
ISBN 0-933849-46-X   Full Color

by Shintaro Maeda, age 8
Wichita, Kansas
ISBN 0-933849-51-6   Full Color

by Miles MacGregor, age 12
Phoenix, Arizona
ISBN 0-933849-52-4   Full Color

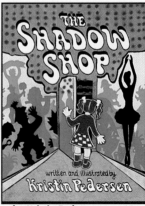
by Kristin Pedersen, age 18
Etobicoke, Ont., Canada
ISBN 0-933849-53-2   Full Color

Travis Williams
age 16

Anika D. Thomas
age 13

Isaac Whitlatch
age 11

Elizabeth Haidle
age 13

Miles MacGregor
age 12

Jayna Miller
age 19

Jonathan Kahn
age 9

Stacy Chbosky
age 14

David McAdoo
age 12

Amity Gaige
age 16

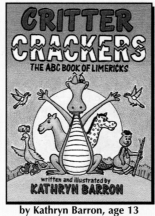

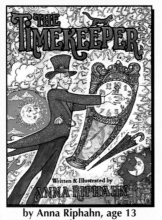

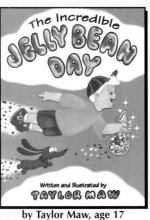

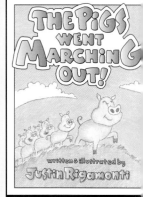